The Bluest Eye

Lightbox Literature Studies

Tammy Gagne and Katie Gillespie

LIGHTBOX
openlightbox.com

LIGHTBOX

Go to **www.openlightbox.com** and enter this book's unique code.

ACCESS CODE

LBXJ3772

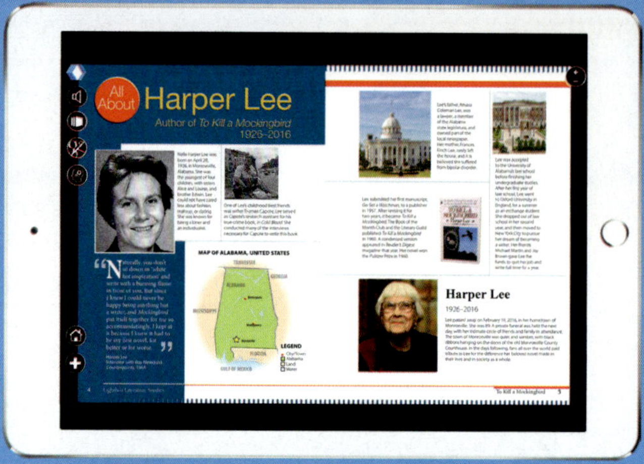

Lightbox is an all-inclusive digital solution for the teaching and learning of curriculum topics in an original, groundbreaking way. Lightbox is based on National Curriculum Standards.

STANDARD FEATURES OF LIGHTBOX

AUDIO High-quality narration using text-to-speech system

VIDEOS Embedded high-definition video clips

ACTIVITIES Printable PDFs that can be emailed and graded

WEBLINKS Curated links to external, child-safe resources

SLIDESHOWS Pictorial overviews of key concepts

TRANSPARENCIES Step-by-step layering of maps, diagrams, charts, and timelines

INTERACTIVE MAPS Interactive maps and aerial satellite imagery

QUIZZES Ten multiple choice questions that are automatically graded and emailed for teacher assessment

KEY WORDS Matching key concepts to their definitions

MORE Extra information and details on the subject

FIRST HAND Letters, diaries, and other primary sources

DOCS Speeches, newspaper articles, and other historical documents

Contents

The Bluest Eye
a novel by
Toni Morrison
WINNER OF THE NOBEL PRIZE

RUBRIC

Conducting an Interview

Students will conduct an interview with a community member about a time period in their community's history, and submit an audio recording and transcript of the interview. An exemplary interview will meet the following criteria.

- Clearly defines the purpose of the interview
- Conducts thorough background research to inform the focus of the interview and the questions
- Drafts a complete list of thoughtful, in-depth, and varied questions prior to the interview
- Interviews a subject with relevant knowledge on the topic and time period in question
- Asks questions in a logical order, building upon each other
- Treats the interview subject in a polite, respectful, and professional manner
- Does not interrupt or rush the interview subject
- Shows interest and enthusiasm in responses and follow-up questions
- Chooses follow-up questions that demonstrate active listening
- Asks for clarification and further details when necessary
- Asks questions about personal experiences related to the topic
- Asks questions regarding factual information and the interview subject's opinion on the topic
- Asks creative questions that reflect fresh insights on the topic
- Records the full interview in a quiet environment
- Organizes and edits the interview transcript to be clear and factual

All About

Toni Morrison

Author of *The Bluest Eye*
1931–

Toni Morrison was born Chloe Anthony Wofford on February 18, 1931, in Lorain, Ohio—a steel town about an hour west of Cleveland. She was the second of George and Ramah Wofford's four children. Both Morrison's father, and her grandfather before him, had faced racism and economic struggles in the South years earlier. They hoped that moving their families to the North would provide them with more opportunities.

"So you've got the most vulnerable people in the world, which are children—female children, female black children—who have never held center stage in anything. If they appear in a book, they're a joke or, you know, just some color or local color or a little walk-on part—the least important. Now black women have sometimes held center stage in some books by blacks, even sometimes by whites, but then, you know, they were maids, cooks, housekeepers—they were really running [things], but the children, they were always lesser. So I wanted to have a little hurt black girl at the center of this story."

Toni Morrison, Interview, National Visionary Leadership Project, 2004

MAP OF THE NORTHEASTERN UNITED STATES

Morrison grew up hearing horrific accounts of racial injustices in the South, but her family also made sure she heard more hopeful stories about the Underground Railroad and other African American triumphs. Her family was filled with positive role models, many of them women, so Morrison grew up with great confidence in her abilities. However, despite the fact that Lorain was a multicultural area of Ohio, Morrison was still subjected to prejudice there.

Morrison graduated with honors from Lorain High School in 1949. She went on to attend Howard University in Washington, D.C., the following autumn, which was also when she began going by the name Toni instead of Chloe.

After receiving her bachelor's degree in 1953, Morrison went on to earn a master's degree in English from Cornell University two years later. She spent several years teaching English, first at Texas Southern University, and later back at Howard University.

It was while teaching at Howard that she met an **architect** named Harold Morrison, the man who would become her husband. The couple married in 1958, and had their first child, Harold, in 1961. Morrison also joined a monthly writing group in which she began writing the story that would evolve into her novel, *The Bluest Eye*. In 1963, when Morrison was expecting her second child, she made the decision to end her marriage.

Following the birth of her son Slade, Morrison moved to New York City where she took a job as a book editor to support herself and her young children. She continued writing *The Bluest Eye* while her children were asleep. It would be the first of several novels for this prolific author. In 1993, Morrison became the first African American to win the Nobel Prize for Literature.

ACTIVITIES

Google Maps

Lorain, Ohio

Explore Toni Morrison's hometown using street view. Lorain, Ohio, is also the setting of *The Bluest Eye*.

First Hand

Interview Toni Morrison: 'I want to feel what I feel. Even if it's not happiness'

Examine this interview with Toni Morrison by Emma Brockes, published in *The Guardian* on April 13, 2012.

1. What types of questions does the interviewer ask? What topics does she focus on? Why would she focus on these specific areas?
2. Brockes notes that Morrison's historical subject matter "gives her a kind of timelessness." Do you think this is an accurate assessment? What parallels can you draw between this observation and *The Bluest Eye*? Give examples from the novel.

RUBRIC

Researching for a Writing Assignment

Students will complete a thorough research process to prepare for a writing assignment, and organize their research in a logical manner that supports their writing. An exemplary research process will meet the following criteria.

- Creates a goal for the research, based on the topic and working thesis
- Creates specific, thoughtful, and inventive research questions that are relevant to the topic of the writing assignment
- Produces a list of categories, key words, and related ideas to effectively assist in researching
- Uses high-quality sources that pertain to the topic and come in a variety of formats, such as books, journals, primary sources, websites, and databases
- Determines accuracy of all sources
- Uses sources that provide balanced research and various perspectives on the topic in question
- Takes notes to highlight the key facts and ideas in order to answer all research questions
- Extracts relevant, detailed information from the sources during the note-taking process
- Organizes the research notes in a clear and concise manner
- Organizes the research notes logically and in a way that sets up the information and ideas for analysis and the writing process
- Analyzes the information and produces ideas and points to support the working thesis
- Uses an effective and suitable format to present all research
- Properly cites all sources used

Setting of the Novel

Morrison set *The Bluest Eye* in her hometown of Lorain, Ohio. She likely chose this setting due to her familiarity with the area, but it also serves to illustrate some of the struggles her characters face. For instance, she mentions an abandoned building on the corner of Broadway and Thirty-fifth Street, which was once a store, as a means of showing the reader that Lorain is not prosperous when the story takes place. Visitors wonder why it has not been torn down, while people who reside in the town simply look away when they walk by it. The building is now the makeshift home of a mother, father, and two children, one of whom is Pecola Breedlove, the story's main character.

Snapshot

The Great Migration

During the **Great Migration**, more than **500,000** African Americans moved from the South to northern states, seeking **better jobs** and **improved race relations**.

Thousands of African Americans settled in **Cleveland**, a city about **30 miles** east of Lorain, Ohio. (48 kilometers)

In **1910**, African Americans made up just **3 percent** of Ohio's population. By **1930**, this had **increased** to **5 percent**.

The Store

"The large 'store' area was partitioned into two rooms by beaverboard planks that did not reach to the ceiling. There was a living room, which the family called the front room, and the bedroom, where all the living was done. In the front room were two sofas, an upright piano, and a tiny artificial Christmas tree which has been there, decorated and dust-laden, for two years. The bedroom had three beds: a narrow iron bed for Sammy, fourteen years old, another for Pecola, eleven years old, and a double bed for Cholly and Mrs. Breedlove. In the center of the bedroom, for the even distribution of heat, stood a coal stove."

Narrator, Autumn

Unique details can often make a fictional story seem more realistic. Morrison's real-life experiences in Lorain enabled her to give *The Bluest Eye* a particular authenticity. She utilizes small, yet accurate details about the physical setting to help tell her story.

Morrison knew that marigolds blossomed in this region of the United States every fall. One of the book's characters—a grown woman named Claudia MacTeer—also knows this, but she remembers an autumn from her childhood when none of the flowers bloomed. Claudia connects this bizarre event to a central and ominous part of the story, something so unimaginable that the only way the story's young characters could cope with it was by believing they could control it with magic.

ACTIVITIES

Video

Toni Morrison: Segregation and Racism in Lorain, Ohio

Find out more about Morrison's experiences growing up in Lorain, Ohio, by watching this video.

1. In the video, Morrison discusses segregation and racism in her hometown, claiming that although there were no laws, there were "understandings." How might the childhood events she describes have impacted the way she portrays Lorain, Ohio, in *The Bluest Eye*? Give textual evidence to support your answer.
2. Why was Lorain chosen as the setting for this story? How do you think the novel would be different if it were set in another city or in another country? Why?

First Hand

'I Regret Everything': Toni Morrison Looks Back On Her Personal Life

Learn more about Morrison's childhood in this National Public Radio interview from April 20, 2015.

1. Morrison describes her hometown as place where racial lines were not very pronounced, claiming that she "didn't really have a strong awareness of segregation and the separation of races until [she] left Lorain," and that she "thought the whole world was like Lorain." How is this exemplified in the novel?
2. Do you think it is possible for Morrison to separate the real-life Lorain, Ohio, from the fictional setting of her novel? Why or why not?

Time Period of the Novel

The Bluest Eye is set in the early 1940s, when Morrison herself was roughly the same age as the character Claudia MacTeer. Similarities can be seen between the fictional MacTeer family and Morrison's real-life family, both of whom struggled to survive during the Great Depression, a decade-long economic **recession**. Money is tight for the MacTeers, and even though Claudia and her sister are just children, the family expects them to do their part to help out by collecting pieces of coal that have fallen off the nearby railroad cars. Although they do not struggle as badly as Pecola's family, the simple task of keeping their home warm enough is challenging for the MacTeers.

Life at the Breedloves' Home

"No one had given birth in one of the beds—or remembered with fondness the peeled paint places, because that's what the baby, when he learned to pull himself up, used to pick loose. No thrifty child had tucked a wad of gum under the table. No happy drunk—a friend of the family, with a fat neck, unmarried, you know, but God, how he eats!—had sat at the piano and played 'You Are My Sunshine.'"

Narrator, Autumn

The Bluest Eye takes places amidst drastic poverty, and the **alcoholism** and violence that can often accompany such severe deprivation. With the Great Depression as its backdrop, *The Bluest Eye* depicts two families who deal with these struggles in significantly different ways. Pecola's parents—and by extension, Pecola herself—are virtually destroyed by their circumstances. The MacTeers, however, manage to create a more positive environment in which the family makes the best of the little they have.

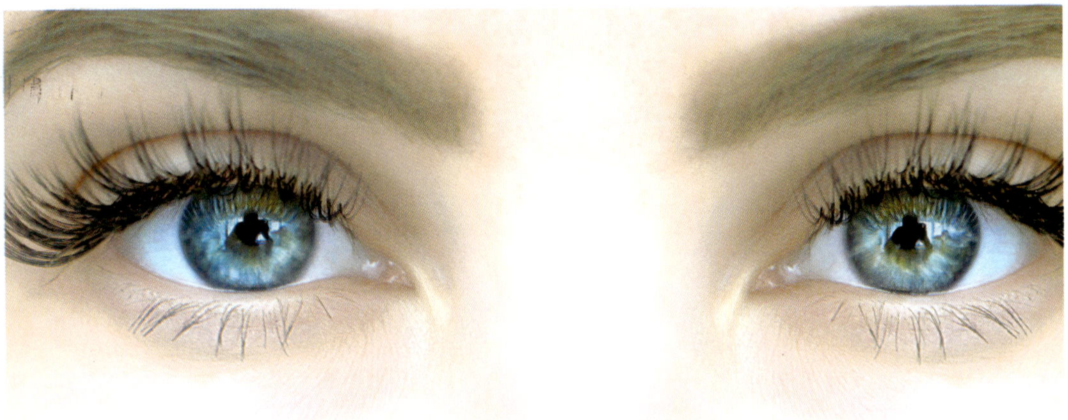

Morrison has said that her inspiration to write the character of Pecola can be traced back to when she herself was a young girl, when an African-American classmate in elementary school confided to Morrison that she longed to have blue eyes. She always remembered the conversation, seeing her friend's wish as form of self-loathing. She wondered what had happened in the little girl's life to make her think that she would be somehow better if she had blue eyes instead of brown.

In the 1960s, a movement began to empower African Americans. After being told for so long that they were ugly, or otherwise less than whites, many African Americans began using the phrase, "Black is Beautiful," during this time period. When Morrison heard the phrase, it always reminded her of her childhood friend, who clearly thought that beauty was linked to this feature most often possessed by whites.

ACTIVITIES

Video

Toni Morrison Talks About Her Motivation For Writing

Discover Morrison's opinion on the "Black is Beautiful" movement by watching this video.

1. In the video, Morrison expresses her concern that people might forget what things were like before the "Black is Beautiful" movement. How does *The Bluest Eye* serve as a reminder "that it wasn't always beautiful," as Morrison puts it? Why is this important?
2. How did the time period that *The Bluest Eye* was written in impact Morrison's creation of the novel? In what ways might the story be different if it were written today?

Weblink

Ghosts in the House
How Toni Morrison fostered a generation of black writers.

Review the *New Yorker* article by Hilton Als published on October 27, 2003.

1. In the article, Als explains that Morrison's novel "came at a time when the prevailing sensibility in most American novels was urban and male." How would Morrison's unique perspective have been received by the public? Why do you think this is the case?
2. Als describes *The Bluest Eye* as having "the white world at the periphery," with "black life...at the center, and black females...at the center of that." Why was this significant at the time? Is this fact still noteworthy today?

Conflict in the Novel

Novels are based on some type of conflict, a struggle between the book's characters and other forces in the story. It is not unusual for a protagonist to face multiple setbacks as part of the story's conflict. Many of these problems come from the story's antagonist, who works against the main character in some way. Conflict may also be the result of other forces, such as society as a whole, or even the main character's internal struggle.

The Four Major Types of Conflict in Literature

MAN vs. MAN

In a man versus man conflict, the protagonist is pitted against another character, called the antagonist. Robert Louis Stevenson's *Treasure Island* is a classic adventure story that features such a conflict. This conflict is between the protagonist, a young boy named Jim Hawkins, and the antagonist, a notorious pirate known as Long John Silver.

MAN vs. SELF

In *Divergent* by Veronica Roth, Beatrice Prior must join a group called a **faction**, based on the strongest aspect of her personality. After choosing a faction, she tries desperately to live her life within its limits, but struggles with herself over this decision. Beatrice also learns about other types of conflict that are arising as a result of the faction lifestyle.

MAN vs. SOCIETY

Man versus society conflict appears in *The Giver*, by Lois Lowry. Jonas lives in what seems to be an ideal community, but is actually a **dystopian** world. Only the Receiver knows what life was like before, and passes on this knowledge to the next person to fulfill this role. After Jonas is chosen to be the Receiver, he sees that his world is not as perfect as everyone thinks, and must decide if he should try to change it.

MAN vs. NATURE

In *The Martian* by Andy Weir, astronaut Mark Watney is the first person to be left behind on Mars when his fellow crew members make an emergency departure during a life-threatening dust storm. Thinking he is dead, they do not look back, leaving Watney to figure out how to live on Mars and get them to come back for him. He must battle against the harsh elements on the **inhospitable** planet in order to survive.

RUBRIC

Writing a Short Story

Students will choose an excerpt from the novel and use it as their inspiration in writing a short story. An exemplary short story will meet the following criteria.

- Engages the reader from the opening line
- Establishes a clear, consistent point of view
- Introduces a narrator and a setting
- Develops an engaging conflict at the heart of the narrative to build tension and keep the reader interested
- Develops characters and events through purposeful and well-crafted literary devices
- Creates a logical progression of events in the narrative that build upon each other using various techniques
- Explores ideas, concepts, and writing styles with creativity and originality
- Demonstrates a high level of skill in using appropriate narrative techniques to tell the story
- Concludes the narrative in a thoughtful, effective manner appropriate to the narrative
- Uses varied, purposeful diction and syntax to affect style and serve the narrative
- Writes with clarity, imagination, and a unique, personal voice
- Does not use stereotypes or clichés
- Uses effective, believable dialogue
- Uses correct spelling, grammar, and punctuation

Types of Conflict in *The Bluest Eye*

The two main types of conflict in *The Bluest Eye* are man versus man and man versus society. Each of these conflicts propels the story forward.

Man versus Man

"Mama had told us two days earlier that a 'case' was coming—a girl who had no place to go. The county had placed her in our house for a few days until they could decide what to do, or, more precisely, until the family was reunited. We were to be nice to her and not fight. Mama didn't know 'what got into people,' but that old Dog Breedlove had burned up his house, gone upside his wife's head, and everybody, as a result, was outdoors."

Claudia, Autumn

Man versus Society

"There is a difference between being put *out* and being put out*doors*. If you are put out, you go somewhere else; if you are outdoors, there is no place to go. The distinction was subtle but final. Outdoors was the end of something, an irrevocable, physical fact, defining and complementing our metaphysical condition."

Claudia, Autumn

Claudia

ACTIVITIES

More

The Types of Conflict in *The Bluest Eye*

Analyze the excerpts from the novel revealing the types of conflict as they appear in *The Bluest Eye.*

1. How do these excerpts of conflict reveal the novel's theme? How do they reveal character? Explain and defend your ideas.
2. Write an analysis of Morrison's development of conflict between Pecola and her parents. What deeper truths may be suggested about these characters as a result of their conflict?

Weblink

What is a Story? Conflict—The Foundation of Storytelling

Examine the *Script* article about conflict in literature.

1. What makes Pecola unique in the way she handles conflict? How do the other characters in the story create conflict for Pecola? Explain why you think Morrison chose to have her characters behave this way, and what effect this has on the reader's opinions of them.
2. How does Pecola respond to the "fight or flight" aspect of conflict? Does this change over the course of the novel? Why do you think this is the case?

RUBRIC

Holding a Classroom Debate

Students will form groups and prepare arguments for a debate on a controversial issue. Exemplary performance in a debate will meet the following criteria.

- Demonstrates in-depth understanding of the topic and related information
- Presents strong, logical, and convincing arguments
- Communicates in a clear and confident manner
- Maintains eye contact
- Uses clear vocal tone and a reasonable rate of vocal delivery
- Uses respectful and appropriate language and body language
- Delivers arguments, evidence, and counter-evidence in an engaging and persuasive manner
- Supports each major point of an argument with several relevant and detailed facts and examples
- Connects all arguments to the overall topic in a clear, concise, and organized manner
- Presents the arguments and supporting evidence in a clear, logical manner
- Presents clear, thorough, and accurate information throughout the debate
- Addresses all of the opposing team's arguments with counter-arguments
- Identifies any weakness in the opposing team's arguments
- Constructs strong and relevant counter-arguments using accurate information
- Presents strong and persuasive arguments throughout the debate
- Summarizes the arguments in the closing statement

Introducing the Characters

A novel's characters are among the most important components of its story. Readers become invested in the plot because they care about what happens to these fictional people. Authors introduce readers to characters in several ways. A common method is telling the reader about them directly, describing their appearances and personalities. A writer can also show the reader who the characters are through their words and actions. Readers can learn about a character through the words of other characters as well.

Major Characters in *The Bluest Eye*

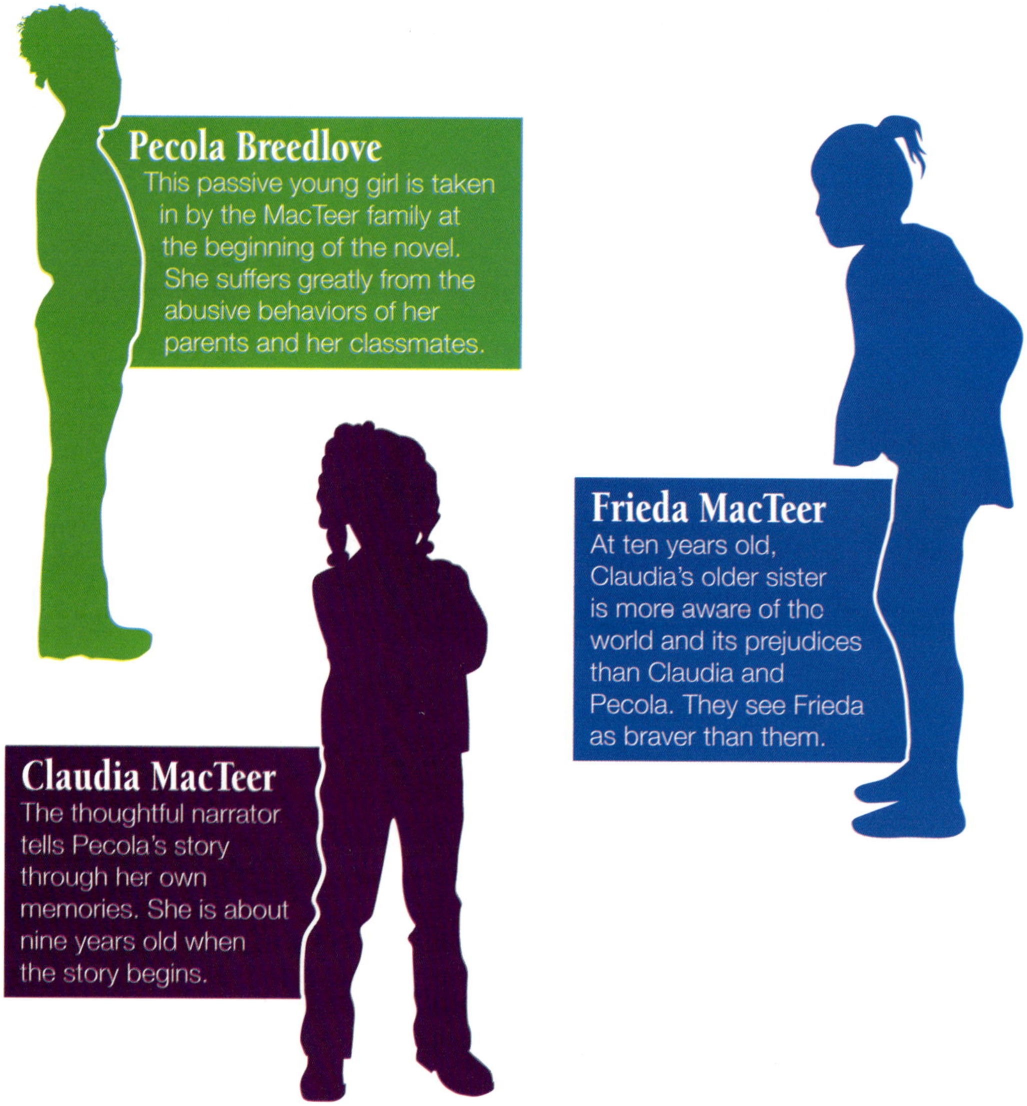

Pecola Breedlove

This passive young girl is taken in by the MacTeer family at the beginning of the novel. She suffers greatly from the abusive behaviors of her parents and her classmates.

Frieda MacTeer

At ten years old, Claudia's older sister is more aware of the world and its prejudices than Claudia and Pecola. They see Frieda as braver than them.

Claudia MacTeer

The thoughtful narrator tells Pecola's story through her own memories. She is about nine years old when the story begins.

Morrison introduces the youngest characters in *The Bluest Eye* through Claudia's childhood memories. Morrison also relies on Claudia's narrations to form the first images of Pauline and Cholly in her readers' minds, but since Claudia only knows the most basic information about these characters, Morrison uses the **omniscient** narrator to tell each of these characters' backstories.

Dynamic characters change as the story moves forward. Pecola, for instance, is deeply affected by the abuse she experiences at the hands of her parents and classmates, and their actions cause her to recede into a lonely world where she begins praying for blue eyes. Static characters do not change through the novel, but they are essential for driving the story forward. In some cases, they contribute to the conflict in the novel, as Maureen does when she tells Pecola she is ugly. Other times, static characters represent more positive things, as Mr. and Mrs. MacTeer do. Claudia's parents love their daughters and work hard to protect them, even though they seem cold or harsh at times to the young girls.

Round characters reveal many details about themselves over the course of the narrative. Both Pecola and her brother Sammy fall into this category, but they deal with their difficult home life in opposite ways. Pecola becomes lonely and desperate, and Sammy decides to run away. Flat characters move the story forward in smaller ways. They display a singular personality trait or none at all. Cholly's Great Aunt Jimmy is a flat character. The reader knows only that she raises Cholly when his mother abandons him and that she is in frail health. Without her, though, Cholly's character likely would not have survived to adulthood.

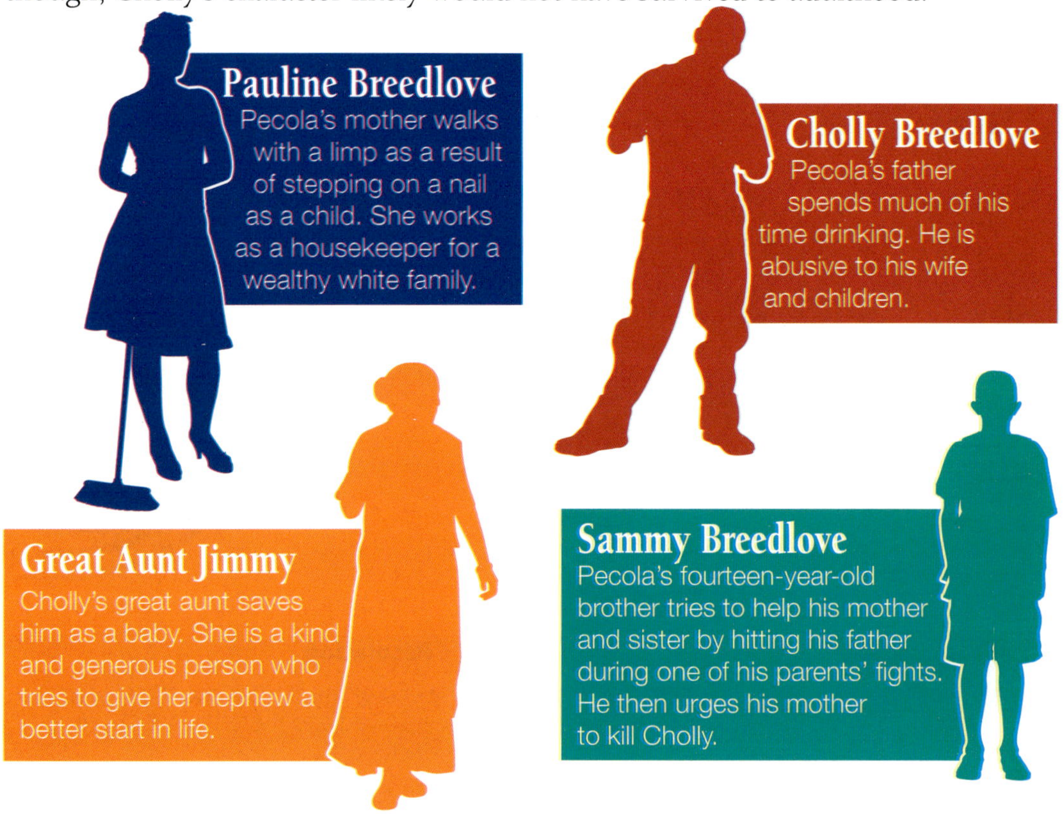

ACTIVITIES

Weblink

Character Analysis of Cholly Breedlove

Review a character analysis of Cholly Breedlove and debate his role in *The Bluest Eye*.

1. Although Cholly commits unforgivable acts, he also inspires sympathy at times, due to the genuine suffering he experiences. How do these contradictory traits affect the reader's opinion of him? Give textual evidence to support your claims.
2. Do you think Cholly is a violent character or a vulnerable character? Is it possible for him to fall into both categories? Why or why not?

More

Character Development in *The Bluest Eye*

Analyze the characters in *The Bluest Eye* using the descriptions on the character map and excerpts from each character. Then, choose a character and answer the following questions.

1. Which of the writer's techniques are most effective at revealing this character's traits? Why?
2. In what ways is the characterization of this character ineffective? What could be done to improve this character's function in the novel? Defend your ideas with evidence.

The Art of Storytelling

Storytelling is an art form that authors can approach in variety of ways. Some authors use their stories to share insight into a broader topic, while keeping the reader's attention focused on the novel's details. While Morrison tells Pecola's story, she addresses the wider topics of racism and abuse, and how these horrible acts affect children who are subjected to them. Another author might tell Pecola's story in a completely different way, but Morrison's style and structure affect the way readers perceive the novel. Writers have many tools, often called literary devices, which they can utilize for this purpose.

Structure of a Narrative

The characters and details of a story make each one different, but most writers use a basic template called Freytag's Pyramid when writing a novel. This structure includes five main components. Morrison followed each of these steps in writing *The Bluest Eye*.

Freytag's Pyramid

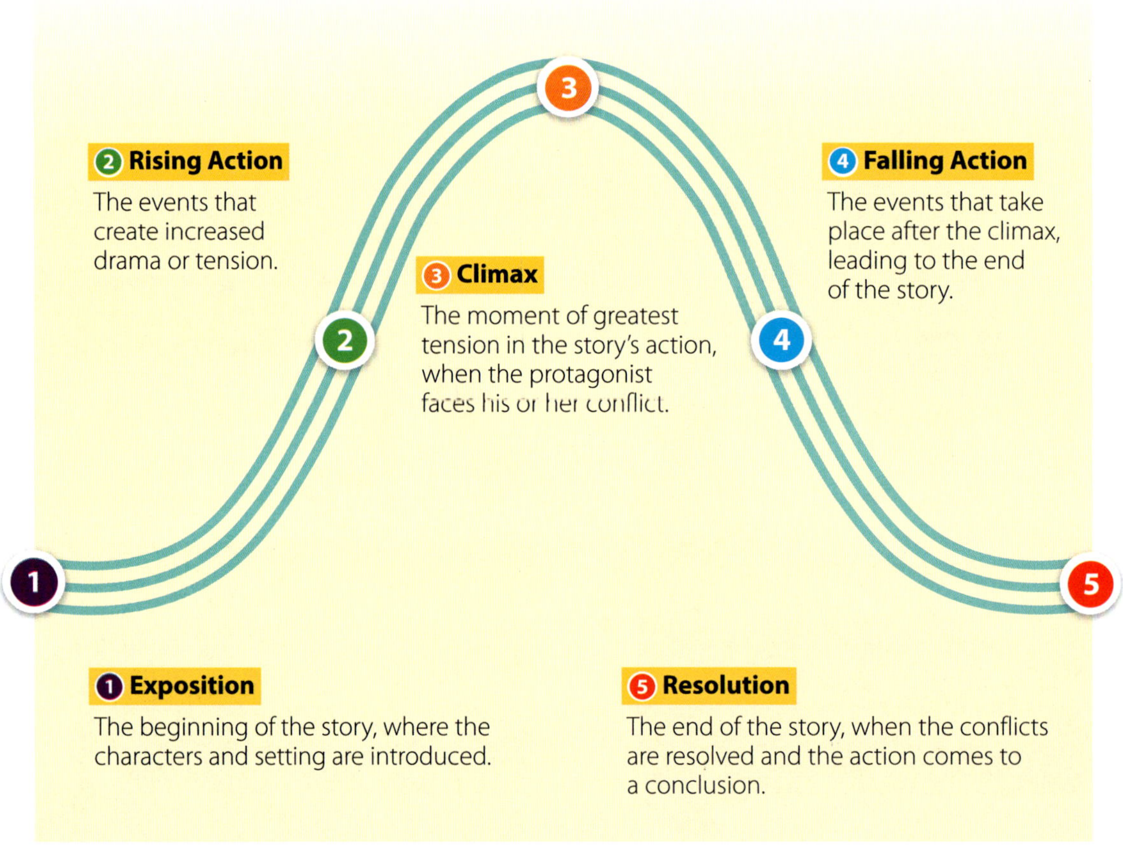

RUBRIC

Creating a Literary Device Analysis Booklet

Students will analyze the author's use of a literary device in the novel, and create a booklet to present this analysis. An exemplary literary device analysis booklet will meet the following criteria.

- Defines the chosen literary device accurately and in detail
- Places the definition of the literary device at the beginning of the booklet
- Provides strong, specific examples of how this literary device is used in the novel
- Describes examples in detail, with quotations properly integrated
- Includes thorough analysis of the use, purpose, and effectiveness of each example of how the chosen literary device is used in the novel
- Arranges all pages logically
- Examples are organized chronologically
- Provides no more than one example and its analysis per page
- Creates a neat, well-organized, and attractive booklet
- Booklet is colorful and displays the student's creativity
- Uses illustrations to represent the chosen literary device and the examples of how it is used in the novel

Plot

Every novel has a plan called a plot. Made up of numerous individual events, the plot moves the story from one point to the next. These events, in order of when they take place, make up the novel's plotline. A well-organized plotline keeps the story on track.

Plot Points in Chapter 1 of *The Bluest Eye*

1. Claudia and her sister collect pieces of coal that have fallen from railroad cars to help heat their home.
2. While gathering the coal one day, Claudia gets sick.
3. Claudia's mother gets angry because her daughter is sick, but Claudia mistakenly thinks she is mad at her.
4. Claudia remembers how her sister made her feel better by singing to her.
5. Claudia and Frieda's mother tells them that they will be renting out a room in their house.
6. The boarder, Henry Washington, impresses the girls with magic tricks.
7. A young girl named Pecola Breedlove also moves into the MacTeer home after her father burns down their house.
8. Pecola adores Shirley Temple, which prompts Claudia to remember how much she hated a white doll she got for Christmas.

Literary Devices

Writers use a variety of literary devices to tell their stories. Most of these devices are either literary elements or literary techniques. The specific literary techniques a writer uses typically depend on the writer's unique style.

Literary Elements

Literary elements are larger features that captivate and engage a reader's imagination. All works of fiction feature various literary elements.

Moral A moral is a lesson that the story offers the reader.

Narrative Point of View The narrative point of view is the perspective from which a story is told.

Action The things that happen in a story are called its action.

Literary Techniques

Literary techniques are the various ways a writer can manipulate language to convey meaning or to create a distinct style.

Rhetorical Questions Rhetorical questions are asked, but they are not expected to be answered.

Simile A simile describes one thing by comparing it to another, typically using the word "as" or "like."

Metaphor The most significant metaphor, or symbol, in *The Bluest Eye* is blue eyes.

ACTIVITIES

Weblink

Toni Morrison: Write, Erase, Do it over

Examine some of Morrison's reflections on writing *The Bluest Eye*.

1. Morrison wrote *The Bluest Eye* in response to the fact that no one had ever written about young black girls, "except as props," before that. What qualities make characters such as Pecola, Claudia, and Frieda more than just "props"? Why is this so important?
2. Morrison tries not to give the reader every detail, believing it is more important to rely on the reader's intelligence and emotions. How is this evidenced in *The Bluest Eye*? Give specific examples from the text.

More

Examples of Literary Techniques from the Novel

Analyze the author's use of literary techniques and how they contribute to the narrative of *The Bluest Eye*.

1. Choose one literary technique used in the novel. In what particular way did the author use this literary technique? How effective was its usage?
2. What arguments can be made for the use of your chosen literary technique in a text? If this technique were overused or underutilized, what effect might it have on an author's work?

Theme in the Novel

A novel's theme is the main idea the author conveys to the reader. This underlying topic can be straightforward, or it may be quite challenging for the reader to identify and fully comprehend. A novel can have several different themes, although one is usually more prominent than the others. In some cases, the reader uncovers the theme along with the characters, an approach which helps the reader identify with the characters as they all learn and grow.

Values

The values of a story's characters have a significant impact on the novel's theme. These beliefs drive the characters' behaviors, both positively and negatively. Just like real people, a novel's characters do not always share the same values, which can often affect the story's conflict. Throughout the course of the novel, a character's values can even change, as the person learns more about the world. Often, the author reveals the characters' values through their actions.

Major Themes of *The Bluest Eye*

Morrison uses her characters' intense experiences and the emotions they evoke to convey several themes to the reader. With the help of these characters, the reader not only sees these themes, but also feels them. It is not just the experiences of the protagonist that accomplish this task. The reader is even given a window into the world of the book's villains, such as Pecola's father, when the narrator tells the story of his sad childhood. The telling of these different stories illustrates such themes as white traits defining the standard of beauty, how the way one is seen affects the way that person sees the world, and the power of narratives.

Claudia

White Traits Defining the Standard of Beauty

"Younger than both Frieda and Pecola, I had not yet arrived at the turning point in the development of my psyche which would allow me to love her. What I felt at that time was unsullied hatred. But before that I had felt a stronger, more frightening thing than hatred for all the Shirley Temples of the world."

Claudia, Autumn

The Way One is Seen Affects How That Person Sees the World

"Each pale yellow wrapper has a picture on it. A picture of little Mary Jane, for whom the candy is named. Smiling white face. Blond hair in gentle disarray, blue eyes looking at her out of a world of clean comfort. The eyes are **petulant**, mischievous. To Pecola they are simply pretty. She eats the candy, and its sweetness is good. To eat the candy is somehow to eat the eyes, eat Mary Jane. Love Mary Jane. Be Mary Jane."

Narrator, Autumn

Pauline

The Power of Narratives

"There I was, five months pregnant, trying to look like Jean Harlow, and a front tooth gone. Everything went then. Look like I just didn't care no more after that. I let my hair go back, plaited it up, and settled down to just being ugly."

Pauline, Spring

Secondary Themes

Other themes in *The Bluest Eye* include coming of age in an abusive environment, and the correlation between poverty, racism, and violence. Cholly, and his behavior toward his daughter, are prime examples of these themes. Cholly's own abusive adolescence leads him to become an abuser himself.

ACTIVITIES

Weblink

How to Identify the Theme in a Literary Work
Evaluate the article discussing what themes are and how to identify them.

1. The writer of the article, Esther Lombardi, cautions readers about confusing theme with the subject of a text. Why is this an important distinction? How might an author's choice of subject influence the themes of a work? Give examples to help explain your answer.
2. According to Lombardi, there are four steps to identifying themes in a published work. How can these steps be applied to *The Bluest Eye*?

More

Major and Secondary Themes
Analyze the author's development of themes over the course of the novel.

1. Choose a secondary theme from this spread and analyze its appearances in the novel. How does this theme first emerge? Which is the most poignant example of this theme in the novel?
2. What particular commentary might the author be making about life as a result of this theme's presence in the text? Explain and defend your ideas.
3. Choose a major theme presented on pages 16–17. In what ways does your chosen secondary theme relate to this major theme? Does it deepen or detract from the major theme? How or in what way?

RUBRIC

Creating a Symbolism Poster

Students will choose one of the other symbols listed on page 19 and analyze its role in the novel. They will then create a poster to present their analysis. An exemplary symbolism poster will meet the following criteria.

- Presents a clear purpose that is conveyed throughout the poster
- Shows an understanding of the concept of symbolism and the role it has in the novel
- Provides an in-depth analysis of what the symbol represents
- Discusses the role the symbol has in the novel
- Clearly indicates where the symbol appears in the novel
- Uses specific, detailed examples from the text to support the analysis
- Makes clear connections to the text
- Properly integrates all quotations
- Organizes the information in a logical, easy-to-read manner
- Includes high-quality graphics that relate to the symbol and effectively enhance understanding of the topic
- Features clear and concise writing
- Uses correct spelling, grammar, and punctuation
- Clearly labels items of importance
- Headings and subheadings are clear and easy to read
- Uses layout to creatively enhances the information
- Creates a poster that is attractive in terms of layout, design, and organization
- Shows a strong effort by the student

Symbolism in the Novel

Symbolism is a literary technique that helps the reader comprehend the themes of the story. Some symbols are physical objects, while others are more conceptual in nature. In certain instances, even words can serve as symbols.

The Marigolds as a Symbol

Claudia uses the marigolds as a symbol for the safety of Pecola's baby. Just as she and Frieda cannot control how the flowers grow, they also cannot decide what will happen with Pecola's pregnancy. Still, they decide to believe that if they do everything just right, the seeds will blossom properly—and that magically, this will help ensure that the baby, too, will be delivered safely. Of course, they have no control over either event, but the flowers that do not appear end up being a symbol of the grim outcome for the infant.

Claudia

The Marigolds

"Quiet as it's kept, there were no marigolds in the fall of 1941...A little examination and much less melancholy would have proved to us that our seeds were not the only ones that did not sprout; nobody's did. Not even the gardens fronting the lake showed marigolds that year. But so deeply concerned were we with the health and safe delivery of Pecola's baby we could think of nothing but our own magic: if we planted the seeds, and said the right words over them, they would blossom, and everything would be all right."

Claudia, Prologue

Blue Eyes as a Symbol

The symbol of blue eyes standing for beauty and happiness is seen in multiple places throughout *The Bluest Eye*. From the white doll that Claudia receives to beloved movie stars, nearly everyone thought to be beautiful in the book shares this predominantly white feature. They also have lighter skin and straighter hair. The symbolism is expressed in the way the characters regard people with these features. Pauline, for instance, prefers the little white girl whose family she works for to her own daughter.

Other Symbols in the Novel

The House

The book begins with a basic description of a house, as told through an early-reader textbook. The house is a symbol of happiness, and represents the stability and love that the fictional family of Dick and Jane have. Although Claudia's house is not perfect, it shares more in common with this house than it does with the store apartment that Pecola lives in with her family.

Cleanliness and Dirtiness

Although Pauline has a reputation for being an excellent housekeeper for the Fisher family, she does not care for her own home in the same way. The contrast between the cleanliness of their home and the dirtiness of her own symbolizes how differently she looks at the two spaces. To her, one is worthy of great effort, while the other is not worth the time.

The Seasons

The story is told in chapters named for the changing seasons, which are also symbols of the events that take place within them. For instance, Claudia recalls being whipped with new switches in spring. Pecola's baby dies in autumn. Morrison connects many events to the time of year in which they take place.

ACTIVITIES

More

What Symbols Appear in the Novel?

Assess the author's use of symbolism in the novel.

1. Choose an example from the chart and analyze what this symbol represents. For which character is this symbol the most poignant in the novel? For which character is the symbol least poignant? Argue your opinions with clear reasons.
2. How is this symbol used or reflected in the novel's themes? Illustrate the ways in which the author's use of language deepens or weakens the meaning of the symbol. Explain and defend your ideas.

Weblink

The Complete Guide to Symbolism

Examine the blog post discussing the usage of symbolism in literature.

1. Contrast and compare examples of analytical descriptions of feelings and sensory descriptions using symbolism from the novel. Which kind is more effective in the novel? Provide reasons for your ideas.
2. Should analytical descriptions play a considerable role in the language of a novel? Why or why not?

The Use of Language

Writers use many different tools to tell their stories. Of all of these tools, language can be one of the most powerful. Authors utilize language in a variety of ways. Some use long, detailed descriptions to introduce the reader to the setting and characters. By describing every sight and sound with words, these authors paint a picture of the novel's world in the reader's mind. Other authors rely on dialogue to show the reader various aspects of their character's personalities and of their reality.

Dialogue and Vernacular

Morrison uses dialogue to relay information, such as how different characters get along or what transpires between them, but she also utilizes it to tell the reader about the characters themselves. For example, when Pauline and Cholly speak, they often use poor grammar. This tells the reader that neither character has had much education. When children speak, they often use words that are not quite right, which tells the reader that they are still learning about life.

Morrison also writes in vernacular, or the dialect that people in a particular area speak. For example, people living in Ohio and those living in Georgia may both speak English, but they often use different words and phrases, and may also pronounce certain words differently. Since Morrison wrote *The Bluest Eye* with different narrators, she used vernacular to help differentiate the voice of each speaker.

Hyperbole

Morrison also uses a type of figurative language called hyperbole in *The Bluest Eye*. This helps convey the intensity of the emotions that the characters experience. Although the reader does not take these exaggerated statements literally, the embellishment is an immediate sign that a character is feeling something powerful. People often use hyperbole in everyday situations, such as, "That box weighs a ton," or "I died of embarrassment."

Pecola's Dandelions

"These and other inanimate things she saw and experienced. They were real to her. She knew them. They were the codes and touchstones of the world, capable of translation and possession. She owned the crack that made her stumble; she owned the clumps of dandelions whose white heads, last fall, she had blown away; whose yellow heads, this fall, she peered into. And owning them made her part of the world, and the world a part of her."

Narrator, Autumn

Personification

Morrison also uses personification to describe physical settings in the book, such as Pecola's home. Although she is talking about a stove, Morrison's depiction of it as a living thing shows how important it is, and the fact that it does not work properly is just another example of how **dysfunctional** the home is, both literally and figuratively.

The Coal Stove

"The only living thing in the Breedloves' house was the coal stove, which lived independently of everything and everyone, its fire being 'out,' 'banked,' or 'up' at its own discretion, in spite of the fact that the family fed it and knew all the details of its regimen: sprinkle, do not dump, not too much....The fire seemed to live, go down, or die according to its own schemata. In the morning, however, it always saw fit to die."

Narrator, Autumn

ACTIVITIES

Document

Call-and-response in *The Bluest Eye*

Review the article by Hong Wu and Liping Yang of Sichuan Agricultural University, exploring Morrison's novel.

1. Who do you think is the intended audience for this document? Why? Are the tone and language used appropriate for this audience? Explain your answer.
2. What are the main points of the document and how are they presented? Are these points conveyed effectively to the reader? Why or why not?

Weblink

What is Hyperbole? Definition and Examples of Hyperboles in Writing

Learn more about the importance and function of hyperbole in literature.

1. How does hyperbole draw attention to a particular point? How would you assess Morrison's use of hyperbole in *The Bluest Eye*? Cite an example from the text and explain why it is effective.
2. It is noted in the article that hyperbole should be used sparingly. Why do you think this is the case? What are the effects when hyperbole is used appropriately?

RUBRIC

Writing a Review

Students will write a review of the novel. An exemplary review will meet the following criteria.

- Grabs the reader's attention with a creative headline
- Begins with an engaging lead to pull the reader into the article
- Introduces the title of the novel, the author, and the genre
- Provides a brief plot description that does not give away the entire story, and makes the reader want to learn more about the novel
- Supports arguments about the novel with accurate and detailed information
- Organizes the review and its arguments in a concise, clear, and logical manner
- Fits the format and style of a review
- Follows the conventions of print or online journalism
- Demonstrates creativity in their approach
- Writes with a unique, engaging voice and perspective
- Provides fresh insight into the novel
- Provides an honest, authentic opinion on the novel
- Gives a clear recommendation on the novel, backed up by specific textual evidence
- Uses correct spelling, grammar, and punctuation

Impact of the Novel at the Time of Publishing

When *The Bluest Eye* was released in 1970, it stood out among other novels, most significantly because it offered a perspective not seen in most young adult fiction of the day. Morrison did not merely discuss racism, but rather showed how it could change a person's perception of both the world and oneself. The novel also addressed several other difficult topics. Many people were uncomfortable with the **explicit** nature of Morrison's text. Some people thought *The Bluest Eye* should be banned, and worked hard to make that censorship a reality. Reviews of the book were mixed. Although the novel had its share of critics, it also received acclaim from the literary community.

High Praise for a First Novel

A review of *The Bluest Eye*, which appeared in *The New York Times* in 1970, praised Morrison's first novel. It claimed, "Miss Morrison exposes the negative of the Dick-and-Jane-and-Mother-and-Father-and-Dog-and-Cat photograph that appears in our reading primers, and she does it with a prose so precise, so faithful to speech and so charged with pain and wonder that the novel becomes poetry."

Message Received

Some publications praised Morrison's narrative techniques and other literary elements, while others spent more time focusing on her novel's message. In a 1971 issue of *Essence*, reviewer Sharon J. Skeeter pointed out that Pecola's tragic situation occurs, "because of direct, as well as subtle, racism." Reviews in *Black World* and *Freedomways* also expressed their reactions to the novel's themes. Many African Americans could relate to the characters and setting Morrison had created.

Taboo Subjects

In addition to racism, the characters in *The Bluest Eye* grapple with other serious issues, such as domestic violence. These were not common subjects for novels during the 1970s. Not everyone thought *The Bluest Eye* was appropriate for teenage readers. In the years since its first printing, many school departments have banned the book from their classrooms. Although some might think that book banning is a thing of the past, *The Bluest Eye* continues to show up on banned lists around the country. In 2013, the president of the Board of Education in Ohio declared that the novel was not appropriate for high school students due to its explicit language and depictions of mature subjects.

Misnamed

A senior editor at Random House in New York, Morrison was also a single mother of two young boys. After she put her children to bed each night, she would stay up late to work on her novel. When the book was first published, Morrison was not happy. She is quoted as saying, "I was upset. They had the wrong name: Toni Morrison... Well, I sort of knew it was going to happen. I was in a daze. I sent it in that way because the editor knew me as Toni Morrison. I write all the time about being misnamed. How you got your name is very special. My mother, my sister, all my family call me Chloe. It was Chloe, by the way, who went to Stockholm... to get the Nobel Prize."

*By **1974**, the novel was **out of print**, although it would be re-released in the future.*

The Bluest Eye was added to **Oprah Winfrey's television book club** in **2000**.

It took Morrison about **five years** to write ***The Bluest Eye***.

ACTIVITIES

Document

The New York Times Book Review of The Bluest Eye

Analyze the review by John Leonard, published on November 13, 1970, exploring his views on *The Bluest Eye*.

1. In the review, Leonard refers to *The Bluest Eye* as poetry. What makes the book poetic? Give specific examples from the novel.
2. According to Leonard, "Morrison's angry sadness overwhelms." Do you agree with this description? If so, what effect do you think this has on the reader? If not, provide a more accurate description, citing evidence from the text to support your position.

First Hand

TONI MORRISON

Examine this interview with Toni Morrison by Christopher Bollen, published in *Interview Magazine* on May 1, 2012.

1. In the interview, Morrison confirms that some of her earliest critics of the novel were from the black community, stating that "they hated it." Why do you think this might have been the case?
2. Morrison goes on to say that most people were initially dismissive of *The Bluest Eye*. How has the way the book is perceived by the public changed over time? Why? Compare and contrast its initial reception with the way it is viewed today.

RUBRIC

Analyzing a Video

Students will watch and assess a video related to a component of the novel, and write an analysis of the video. An exemplary video analysis will meet the following criteria.

- Identifies the purpose of the video
- Identifies the intended audience of the video
- Describes how the content of the video is presented
- Summarizes the information and opinions presented in the video
- Analyzes the quality of the content presented in the video
- Assesses the effectiveness of the video
- Discusses the technical aspects of the video and whether or not these enhance the content
- Determines whether the images and graphics used in the video relate to the content
- Determines whether the video is easy to follow and understand
- Gives the analysis a clear and consistent purpose
- Organizes the analysis in a logical, effective manner
- Presents a strong, clear argument about the video
- Provides strong and accurate details to support the argument about the video
- Considers other perspectives on the purpose and effectiveness of the video
- Makes connections between the video and the novel
- Properly integrates quotations from the video
- Cites all sources used in the analysis

Impact of the Novel Now

Although it is now considered a classic, *The Bluest Eye* continues to attract its share of controversy. Morrison has also earned a reputation for tackling subjects that most writers do not, and she does so with a fierce candor that contributes to her unique voice. Following the publication of her first novel, Morrison went on to write several more books, including *Sula*, *Song of Solomon*, and *Beloved*. They, along with *The Bluest Eye*, are often studied in high school classrooms. *The Bluest Eye* has even been added to the reading list of Common Core State Standards, which is used in many states, though many parents and legislators still try to keep it from reaching students' hands, due to its uncomfortable content.

First editions of *The Bluest Eye* can sell for **$3,000 to $10,000**.

In **2014**, the American Library Association ranked *The Bluest Eye* among the **Top 10 Most Challenged Books**.

The Bluest Eye sold **800,000** copies after Oprah added the novel to her popular book club, **30 years after** the novel's original release.

Prompting Important Discussions

Shekema Silveri is the founder and executive director of the Inspiring Future Educators Academy of Teaching & Technology, a school in Atlanta, Georgia, which teaches *The Bluest Eye*. She and her students often discuss why Shirley Temple was so revered in the novel, and why so many African-American children have grown up with blue-eyed, blonde-haired dolls that look nothing like them. "For the vast majority of my life I thought that straight hair or lighter eyes or lighter skin was what beauty was...," Silveri shared with the PBS program, *American Experience*. "That theme of beauty being tied to whiteness—that's something that we've been able to challenge inside the classroom."

Adapting the Story for the Stage

In 2012, *The Bluest Eye* was performed in front of audiences at Northwestern University's Theatre and Interpretation Center as a play. Lydia Diamond, who adapted the novel, won a Black Arts Alliance Image Award for Best New Play at Steppenwolf Theatre. The play was later performed off-Broadway at the New Victory Theater in New York. The welcome reception the work received in play form is evidence that the story is as relevant today as it was when the novel was first published.

Banning the Book

In 2014, *The Bluest Eye* was removed from the assigned reading list at an Ohio high school after a parental complaint about the book's controversial content. Although the book has been banned elsewhere, Morrison herself noted the irony of such an incident occurring in her home state. Morrison observed, "I mean if it's Texas or North Carolina as it has been in all sorts of states. But to be a girl from Ohio, writing about Ohio having been born in Lorain, Ohio. And actually relating as an Ohio person... [it] is ironic at the least."

Black Lives Matter

In 2015, Melissa Harris-Perry wrote an essay on the Black Lives Matter movement in which she quoted *The Bluest Eye*, when Claudia explains, "I felt a need for someone to want the Black baby to live." Harris-Perry later added, "In this moment, I too feel the need for someone to want the Black babies to live. To want Black mothers to celebrate, not grieve. To want Black women to be brides, not widows. To want Black men to thrive, not die. To want Black youth to play, not cower." Through her novel, Morrison helped give future generations a voice to speak out about the race-related problems that continue to plague the world.

ACTIVITIES

Video

Toni Morrison | TIME Magazine Interviews | TIME

Learn more about Morrison and *The Bluest Eye* by watching this video.

1. In the video, Morrison claims that before *The Bluest Eye*, no one had ever taken little black girls seriously in literature. How did the novel help to raise awareness of this issue and encourage that the standards of accurate representation be raised?
2. Morrison is asked if young, black females are still dealing with the same self-acceptance issues as Pecola in *The Bluest Eye*. Do you agree with her response? Why or why not?

Document

THE BLUEST EYE
by Lydia Diamond

Analyze the script by Lydia Diamond for the stage adaptation of *The Bluest Eye*.

1. The play opens the same way as the novel, but the words are spoken by the cast instead of by a narrator, beginning with Pecola and then adding other characters to the chant. Why do you think Diamond has chosen to stage the introduction this way? What is the impact of this on the audience?
2. In the descriptions of the cast, it is noted that the children are to be played by adults in the stage version of the novel. Explain why Diamond might have chosen to have adults play these roles instead of children.

RUBRIC

Creating a Timeline

Students will explore a topic related to the novel and create a timeline to present their research on historical events connected to this topic. An exemplary timeline will meet the following criteria.

- Includes the most significant events pertaining to the topic to be compared and analyzed
- Includes interesting events
- Uses accurate information for all events, including date, location, and major details
- Orders the events in a chronological sequence
- Describes each event with accurate, vivid, and specific details
- Presents the topic from three or more perspectives
- Inspires the reader to ask thoughtful questions regarding the events and perspectives presented in the timeline
- Uses correct spelling, grammar, and punctuation
- Presents the timeline in a visually attractive and striking manner
- Presents the timeline in a neat, organized manner that is logical and easy to follow
- Uses creativity to present the timeline in an engaging manner
- Effectively communicates the historical information relating to the topic
- Supports each event with reliable sources
- Expresses a clear purpose for creating the timeline
- Enhances the reader's understanding of the topic
- Includes a correctly formatted bibliography of all sources used to create the timeline

Perspectives on the White Standard of Beauty

One of the strongest themes in *The Bluest Eye* is that of typically white traits defining the standard of beauty. Morrison drove this point home by showing the reader how a young, innocent child's self-image is destroyed by society, and even by the people who are supposed to love her because they themselves have been victims of this skewed ideal. The fictional Pecola Breedlove could have been any real-life 11-year-old girl growing up in Lorain, Ohio, in 1941.

Timeline of Milestones in Black is Beautiful History

1947 Patty-Jo, the first stylish African-American doll, is designed by Jackie Ormes.

1974 Model Beverly Johnson becomes the first African-American model to appear on the cover of *American Vogue*.

1900s

1960s The Black is Beautiful movement begins.

1990 Carole Anne-Marie Gist becomes the first African-American woman to win the title of Miss USA.

1992 Lana Ogilvie becomes the first black woman to be featured in a major cosmetics company ad campaign when she signs a contract with Covergirl.

Although the story was set 30 years before the book's release, society's standards were just beginning to change from the white ideal to a more inclusive idea of beauty during the 1970s. In the years that followed the novel's publication, society has continued to hold onto the white ideal, evolving slowly and sometimes even taking marked steps back.

1994 Supermodel Iman starts her own cosmetics company for women of color.

2015 The *Washington Post* reports that black women are likely to receive fewer matches and messages from interested parties on dating sites.

2000s

2003 Actress Halle Berry appears on the cover of *People* magazine's "50 Most Beautiful People" issue.

2016 *The New York Times* reports that as many as 70 percent of women in West Africa buy products to bleach their skin.

2017 Several women of color—including Beyoncé, Lupita Nyong'o, and Zoe Saldana —appear on *Esquire* magazine's list of the "25 Most Beautiful Women of All Time."

ACTIVITIES

Transparency–Timeline

Timeline of Milestones in Black is Beautiful History

Examine the historical and cultural contexts shown on the timeline. Then, contrast and correlate its elements with the themes and events presented in *The Bluest Eye.*

1. In what ways can historical events, culture, and social mores influence a population's perspective on beauty standards? How might these elements have shaped the way a reader in the late 1970s interpreted the novel?
2. How might the era in which Toni Morrison wrote *The Bluest Eye* have influenced the novel's themes and settings? Where in the novel is this most evident? Explain your reasoning.
3. Which current events, changes in laws, new ideas, or political discussions are shaping traditional standards of beauty in the United States today? Which ideas and attitudes are still prevailing? Why?
4. How might current events and present perspectives affect the way a reader interprets the novel? Why is it important for readers to understand the era and context in which a novel is written?

RUBRIC

Writing a Comparative Essay

Students will compare two literary devices used in the novel, and then write a comparative essay based on their analysis. An exemplary comparative essay will meet the following criteria.

- Consists of a one-paragraph introduction, three body paragraphs, and a one-paragraph conclusion
- Introduction includes an engaging lead statement about the topic of the essay, more detailed information about the novel, and a one-sentence thesis that specifically states the essay's argument
- Body paragraphs include a topic sentence that refers to the thesis and how the idea appears in the novel, a supporting sentence that points to this part of the novel, textual evidence of this idea from the novel, and analysis of this evidence
- Body paragraphs end with a transition to the next paragraph
- Conclusion refers to the topic of the essay and the three points presented in the body paragraphs, and restates the thesis
- Provides a thorough analysis of the literary devices in question
- Cites strong and thorough textual evidence to support analysis of what the novel says explicitly
- Presents a clear, specific thesis that indicates a high level of critical engagement
- Organizes ideas in a logical manner
- Communicates arguments in a clear, effective manner
- Properly integrates all quotations
- Correctly cites all sources used
- Correctly formats bibliography

Writing a Comparative Essay

The Bluest Eye includes some fascinating characters and themes. After reading the novel, write a comparative essay to contrast how two literary devices are used in the narrative. You may compare two characters, themes, symbols, or settings. Bear in mind that a comparative essay needs a well-formed argument. You must clearly state both the differences and similarities between the two literary devices you choose to explore. Offer evidence for your position using logical thoughts and quotes from the novel as examples.

How to Analyze and Compare Characters

Use the chart below to guide your comparison between two characters in *The Bluest Eye.*

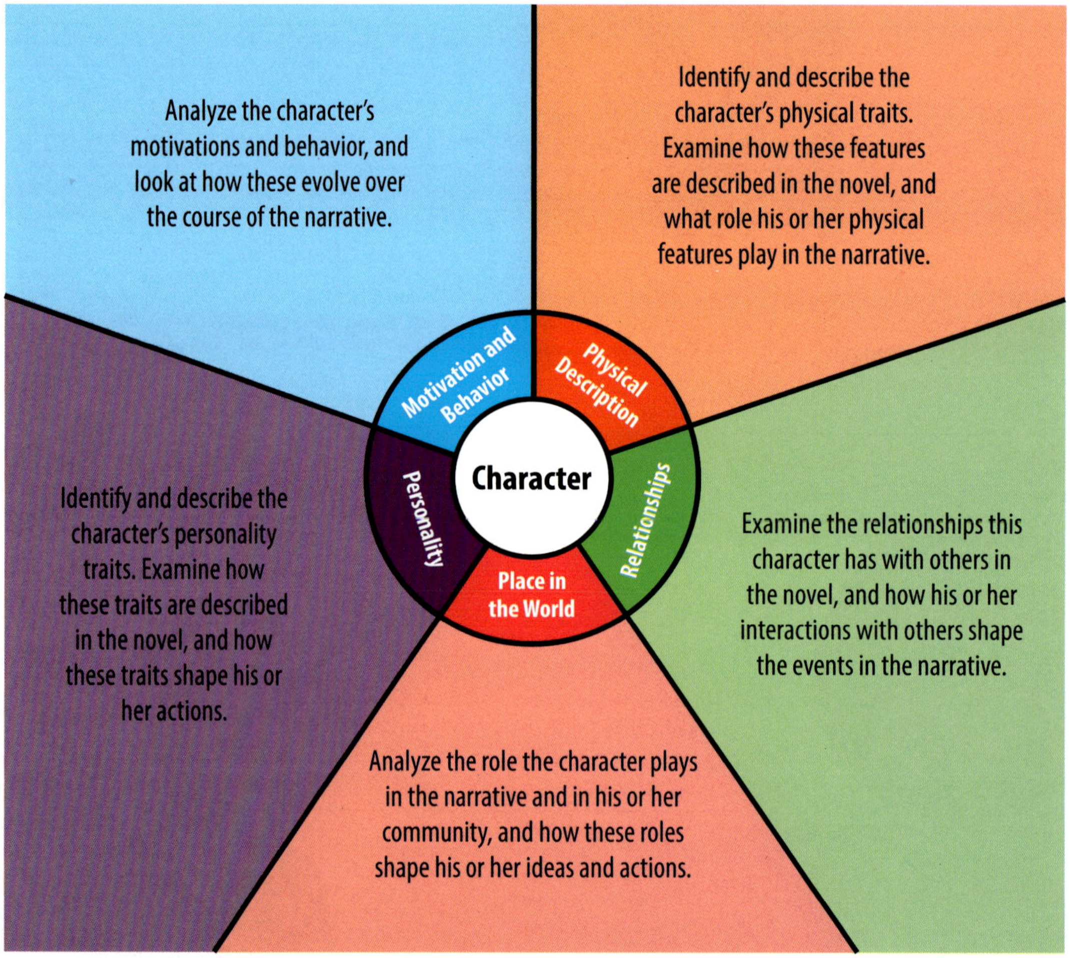

Comparing Pecola and Claudia

Pecola

Personality
- Loves Shirley Temple
- Embraces the white standard of beauty
- Thinks that people are hateful to her because she is ugly

Motivation and Behavior
- Wants to be loved and thinks that having the bluest eyes will help this happen

Place in the World
- Protagonist
- Abused by her parents, boys at school, and society

Relationships
- Daughter of Cholly and Pauline Breedlove
- Sister of Sammy
- Friend of Claudia and Frieda

Physical Description
- Eleven years old
- Entering puberty as the story begins
- African American

Claudia

Place in the World
- Dynamic character in the story
- Tries to help Pecola

Motivation and Behavior
- Hates the white standard of beauty that her sister and friend possess
- Believes that she can help Pecola's baby survive by planting marigolds

Relationships
- Daughter
- Sister of Frieda
- Friend of Pecola

Physical Description
- Nine years old
- African American

Personality
- Frustrated by Pecola's admiration of Shirley Temple
- Hates white baby dolls and little white girls

More

Questions for Character Analysis

Analyze how specific character features, such as conflicts, motivations, relationships, place in the world, and personality affect the plot of *The Bluest Eye*. Cite strong and thorough textual evidence to support your analysis of what the novel says explicitly as well as the inferences you may have drawn from the novel's setting, themes, and symbols.

Quiz Answers

1. B
2. C
3. A
4. C
5. D
6. B
7. A
8. D
9. C
10. C

Key Words

alcoholism: the disease of becoming dependent on alcoholic beverages

architect: a person who designs buildings and other structures

dysfunctional: not working properly or peacefully

dystopian: describing an imaginary state where everything is unpleasant

explicit: stated clearly with extreme frankness and details

faction: an individual group that forms within a larger group

inhospitable: not friendly or accommodating to a person

omniscient: knowing everything

petulant: ill-tempered or rude

recession: a time of great financial hardship for a country

Literary Terms

action: everything that occurs in a narrative

antagonist: the character who stands in opposition to the protagonist; in some cases, the antagonist creates or represents the conflict that the protagonist faces

characterization: the act of describing a character through the person's appearance and personality

climax: the moment of greatest tension in the story's action

conflict: a struggle between two or more opposing forces, creating a tension that must be resolved

dialogue: the words spoken between characters in a story

exposition: the beginning of the story, where the characters and setting are introduced

falling action: the events that take place after the climax, leading up to the end of the story

Freytag's Pyramid: a narrative structure consisting of five elements; this includes exposition, rising action, climax, falling action, and resolution

hyperbole: an exaggerated statement

literary elements: components of every literary work

literary techniques: unique structures of a literary work

metaphor: a symbol used in a story as a literary technique

narrative: a logically arranged series of events presented for an audience; a story

narrator: the character or person telling the story, providing background information and opinions on the events, and connecting the gaps between major events and dialogue

plot: the events that take place in a story

protagonist: the person or thing that acts in opposition to the antagonist

resolution: the end of the story, when the problems are resolved and the action comes to a conclusion

rhetorical question: a question that is asked not to be answered but to make a point

rising action: the events that create increased drama or tension

simile: a comparison between two things using the word "like" or "as"

symbolism: a stylistic device using symbols to represent and intensify concepts and ideas

vernacular: the way people in a particular area speak

Index

LIGHTBOX

SUPPLEMENTARY RESOURCES

Click on the plus icon found in the bottom left corner of each spread to open additional teacher resources.

- Download and print the book's quizzes and activities
- Access curriculum correlations
- Explore additional web applications that enhance the Lightbox experience

LIGHTBOX DIGITAL TITLES

Packed full of integrated media

VIDEOS

INTERACTIVE MAPS

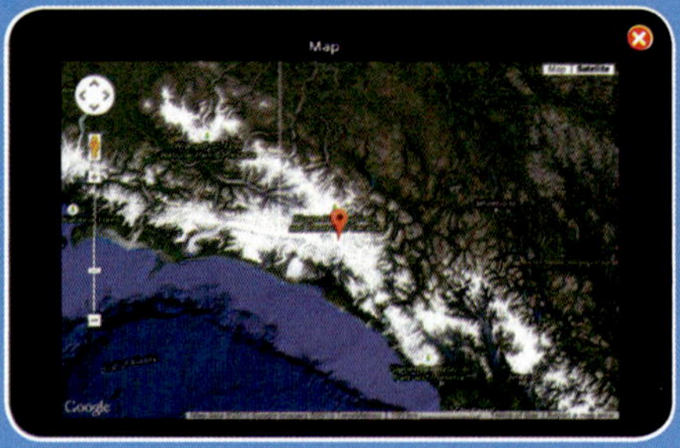

WEBLINKS

SLIDESHOWS

QUIZZES

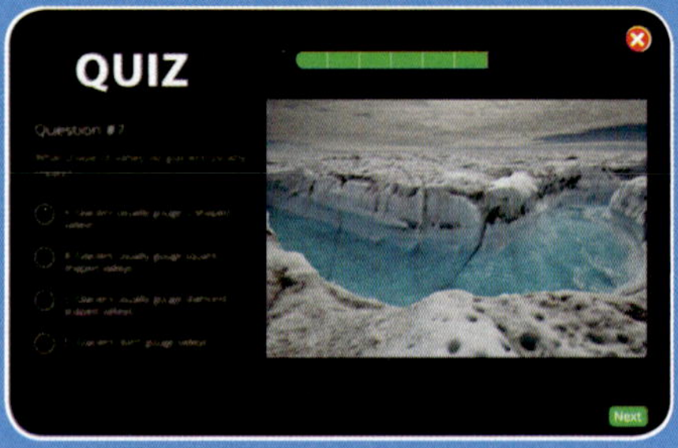

OPTIMIZED FOR

- ✓ TABLETS
- ✓ WHITEBOARDS
- ✓ COMPUTERS
- ✓ AND MUCH MORE!

Published by Smartbook Media Inc.
350 5th Avenue, 59th Floor New York, NY 10118
Website: www.openlightbox.com

Library of Congress Cataloging-in-Publication Data
Names: Gagne, Tammy, author. | Gillespie, Katie, author.
Title: The bluest eye / Tammy Gagne and Katie Gillespie.
Description: New York, NY : Smartbook Media Inc., [2018] | Series: Lightbox literature studies | Includes index.
Identifiers: LCCN 2017054080 (print) | LCCN 2017056327 (ebook) | ISBN 9781510537057 (Multi-User eBook) | ISBN 9781510537040 (hard cover : alk. paper)
Subjects: LCSH: Morrison, Toni. Bluest eye--Examinations--Study guides. |Morrison, Toni. Bluest eye--Juvenile literature.
Classification: LCC PS3563.O8749 (ebook) | LCC PS3563.O8749 B5528 2018 (print) | DDC 813/.54--dc23
LC record available at https://lccn.loc.gov/2017054080

Printed in Brainerd, Minnesota, United States
1 2 3 4 5 6 7 8 9 0 22 21 20 19 18

062018
121017

Editor: Katie Gillespie
Art Director: Terry Paulhus

The publisher acknowledges Getty Images, iStock, Alamy, and Dreamstime as its primary image suppliers for this title.